CLARGE PR

MW01115476

Moonlight M

Arabian Nights

OM KIDZ

An imprint of Om Books International

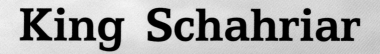

King Schahriar

Sassinadae was an ancient dynasty, which ruled for four hundred years from Persia to China.

One of the Kings was a kind and just man. He had two sons — Schahriar and Schahzeman.

Many years passed, and the King became old. Before he died, he called Schahriar to his bedside and said, "My dear son, from today, this kingdom is yours. Take good care of it." And the old King breathed his last.

Schahriar was married to a lovely queen, who was famous for her beauty. He loved her a lot. One day, Schahriar caught the Queen being unfaithful to him. He was very angry and ordered the Vizier to punish her.

Though the Queen was punished, Schahriar was very sad, as she had betrayed his love.

He became insane in his sadness. Schahriar ordered the Vizier, "All women are the same. They need to be punished! From today, you

will bring a new lady to me every day. I will be married to her at dawn, and she will spend one night with me. The next morning, she will be killed by you."

The Vizier was shocked. He said, "Oh King, you have been loved by your subjects till today. This act of yours will anger and sadden them no end." But the King would not pay heed to the Vizier's words.

From that day, the Vizier would bring a girl to Schahriar every morning. The girl would become his bride and stay in the palace for the day and night. Next morning, the Vizier would kill her.

The whole kingdom was unhappy with Schahriar's act. But nothing could stop his decision. For days, this continued.

The Vizier himself had two daughters. The elder one was called Scheherzade and the younger was called Dinarzade. Scheherzade was pretty and intelligent, while Dinarzade was an ordinary girl.

One evening, the Vizier returned home, tired and unhappy, as he hated the killings he had to do every morning.

Scheherzade went up to her father and said, "Father, I have a solution to bring the King to his senses. But for that you have to listen to me." The Vizier said, "Tell me young one! Anything to stop this bloodshed..."

Scheherzade said, "Father, marry me to the King."

The Vizier was shocked with what he had just heard. He said, "Scheherzade! Are you telling your own father to kill you?"

Scheherzade said calmly, "Father, listen to my plan! You will not have to put me to death. I will interest the King in such a way, that he will not ask you to kill me."

The Vizier said, "That is impossible! The King will never change his mind, whatever you do! I cannot risk your life to stop the King."

Scheherzade said, "Father, think about it. If you agree to what I say, you can save the lives of hundreds of girls. If you do not, you will have to bear the pain of killing them each day."

The Vizier had to finally agree with a heavy heart. Then Scherherzade spoke to her sister, Dinarzade. She said, "Here is my plan... I will persuade the King to allow you to sleep in the

room next to ours. Then, just before sunrise, call me to tell you a story. I will tell you such an interesting story, that the King will want me to be alive to finish it."

Dinarzade agreed to the plan. The next day, the Vizier took Scheherzade to Schahriar. He was surprised, and said, "Why have you brought your own daughter? Don't you know that you will have to put her to death?"

The Vizier replied, "Your Majesty, she is not scared of what awaits her. She has decided to be your bride on her own. I did not force her."

Schahriar agreed after some thought and was married to Scheherzade.

As night approached, Scheherzade said, "I have been very close to my sister. As my last wish, please allow her to sleep in the room next to ours."

Schahriar understood her wish and agreed to what she had asked for. Dinarzade was called to the palace. She was made to sleep in the room next to the royal chamber. Just before sunrise, Dinarzade called out to Scheherzade to tell her a story.

Scheherzade began her most interesting story. Schahriar,

who was also awake, became interested in the story and started listening intently. He forgot all about the sunrise. When he realized, he ordered the guards to give her an extra day, so that she could complete the story.

And thus, Scheherzade had earned her extra day. But her intelligence did not stop there. She continued with interesting stories every night — a thousand and one of them... and they came to be known as the world's most famous collection of stories — The Arabian Nights!

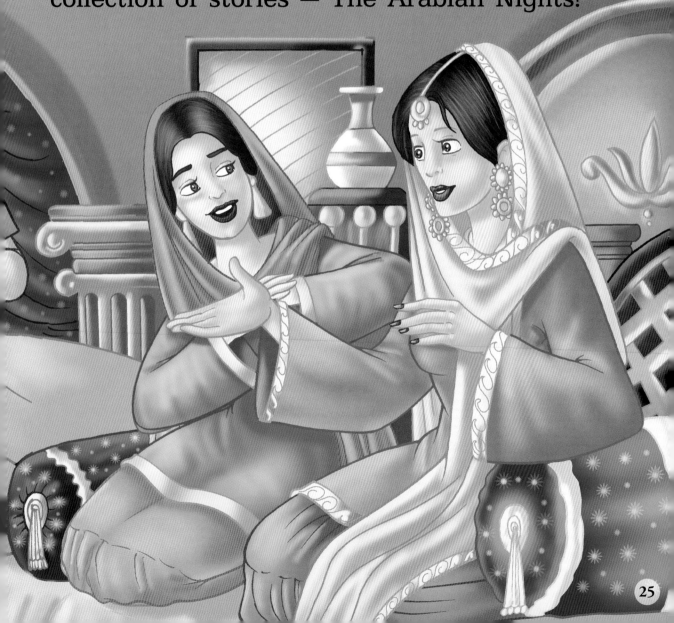

The Greedy Trader

Once upon a time, there lived a rich trader. He was not born rich. His parents had left him a small treasure. But the hard working trader worked day and night to grow his riches. Finally, he was the owner of eighty camels.

He used to lend these camels to merchants, who would carry things from one city to the other using these camels to carry the load.

One day, the trader was walking to a city with all his eighty camels. He stopped at a lonely point, as his camels needed rest. A few minutes later, a saintly looking man appeared from nowhere and sat down next to him.

He looked at the trader and said, "Would you be interested in finding a great fortune?"

The trader was puzzled. The saint went on to explain, "Not far from here, is a hidden treasure. It is so huge that even if you filled the sacks of all your eighty camels, you would still not have taken even a half of it."

The trader was delighted to hear this. He said, "Sir, I can see that the riches of this world mean nothing to you, as you have adopted sainthood. But tell me where this treasure is, and I will fill the sacks of all my

camels and give one camel with the gold to you as a gift."

The saint laughed and said, "Don't you think you are being unjust? Since I am telling you the place where the treasure is, you

should give me half of your camels with the gold." The trader thought for a while. But the saint went on to add, "If you give me half of the camels — forty of them — I will make sure that you get a thousand more." At this the

trader agreed and they both travelled towards the treasure.

They reached a little valley, which was closed from both sides by two mountains. The camels could hardly enter. The saint told the trader, "Ask the camels to lie down." As soon as the camels were on the ground, the saint kindled a fire from dry wood. He then threw a handful of perfumes on it. Suddenly, a huge smoke arose from it.

The saint parted the smoke into two parts and between that emerged a beautiful palace.

The trader rushed inside the palace. When he saw gold lying everywhere, he could not contain himself. He jumped with joy holding

coins and necklaces in his hand. He then loaded all his camels with heaps and heaps of gold. When it was time to leave, the saint picked up a vase lying in a corner of the palace and told the trader, "I am taking this vase. It has a lovely ointment in it."

The trader was not interested in what the saint was saying. He wanted to rush home with all his gold. As agreed, he gave the forty camels to the saint. Both said goodbye to each other and parted ways. When the trader had

gone a few steps, he thought about what a saint could do with forty camels. So he ran back to him after halting his camels.

He told the saint, "Sir, I am sure you are not good at riding camels. It will not be possible for you to handle forty camels. Why don't you give me ten?" The saint did not think for even a second. He agreed and gave the trader ten camels. But the trader's greed did not end with that. He went a few steps

ahead and then again ran back to the saint for ten more camels. This time also the saint did not stop him.

The trader kept doing this till he had all the forty camels that he had given the saint

back with him. Now he thought, "What could be in that vase? I am sure there must be something more valuable than all this in that vase. That is why the saint is carrying it." So he ran back to the saint.

He said, "Sir, would you be kind enough to give me that vase, as I can't imagine what a saint could do with that." The saint happily gave it to him. The trader asked him the powers of the ointment that the vase had. The

saint said, "If you touch your left eye with a little bit of that ointment, then you can see all the hidden treasures in this world. But if you touch your right eye with it, you will go completely blind."

The trader said, "Sir, I can't wait to test the powers of this vase. Please touch my left eye with the ointment." The saint did what the trader had asked him for, and the trader shouted aloud, "I can see! I can see! I can see

every single treasure everywhere in the world.
I am such a lucky man!"

But greed overcame him. He could not
believe that the same ointment could have
two opposite effects on two eyes. So he asked

the saint to touch his right eye also with the ointment.

The saint said, "Son, I am warning you. You will go completely blind. Please do not ask me to do such evil." But the trader insisted. The

saint finally gave up and touched his right eye with the ointment.

The trader went blind in both the eyes. He cried to the saint saying, "Don't you have the powers to reverse the effect of the ointment?" But the saint replied, "Son, it is not the ointment that blinded you, it is your greed!"

"If only you had gone home with your forty camels, you would have been a rich and happy man today. Greed never pays," said the saint.

The Husband and the Honest Parrot

Once upon a time, there lived a loving couple in a beautiful house by the riverside. The husband loved his wife very much.

One day, the husband went to the nearby village for some important work. There he saw the people having fun at a fair.

When he entered the fair, he saw a lot of birds for sale. The husband liked a parrot, which looked special.

The shopkeeper who sold the parrot to the husband said, "This bird is very special, Sir!

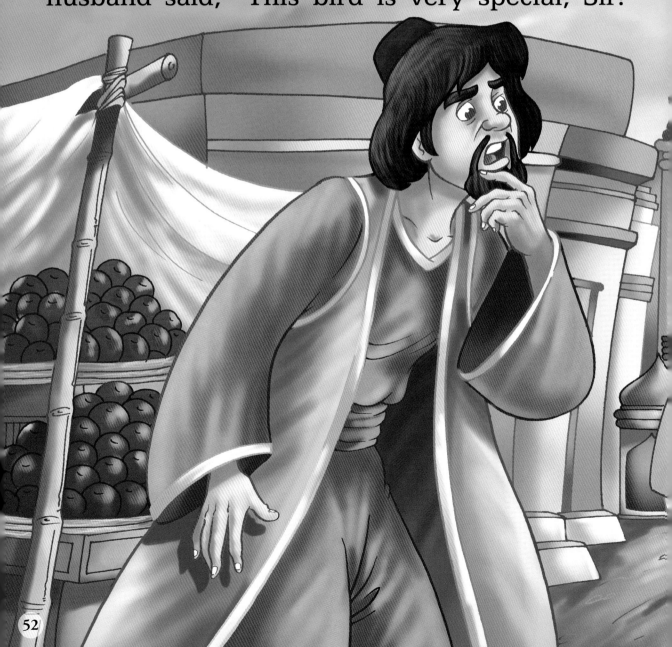

It can speak and can also tell you what it sees during the day."

The husband replied, "I am surprised that a parrot can talk! I am sure that my wife will love it." And he bought the parrot.

When he came home, he told his wife, "Look what a lovely gift I got for you! I will hang it in a corner of the house to remind you of my love." He never told her that the parrot could speak.

In the morning, the husband went out for his work. The parrot kept looking at what the wife did the whole day.

It saw that the wife was very careless and lazy. She burnt the vegetables on the stove while cooking. She let the boiling milk spill over the stove. There were many more such wrong things that the parrot made note of.

When the husband came home in the evening, he went straight to the parrot and asked it quietly, "My lovely pet, what did you see during the day?"

The parrot replied, "Master, I saw the food getting burnt and the milk spilling over the stove." The husband was quite upset with his wife's carelessness. He called her and said,

"How can you be so careless? If you behave in this manner, what will the children follow? Do not repeat your mistake."

The wife was surprised as to who was carrying tales about her. She scolded the servants in the house. But they told her,

"Madam, it is not us. It is the parrot hanging in the cage who is telling your husband things about you."

So the wife decided to punish the parrot. Next day, when the husband was away at work, she told one servant to turn a hand-mill under the bird's cage; another to throw water from above the cage; and the third servant to take a mirror and turn it in front of its eyes—from left to right by the light of a candle.

That evening, when the husband came home, he asked the parrot what it had seen. The innocent parrot said, "I could not see anything as rain, lightning and strong winds were blowing." The husband, who knew that it had been a calm day, decided that the parrot did not understand things well, and was saying the wrong things. He punished the parrot by not giving it food for two days. The poor parrot went hungry.

A few days later, he came back home early from work.

He saw that the kitchen was smoky. The dinner, which was being cooked, was burning. He saw the clothes lying around the house. The house was indeed a mess. The husband was shocked to see his house in such a shape. He had always come back from work to find a beautiful home.

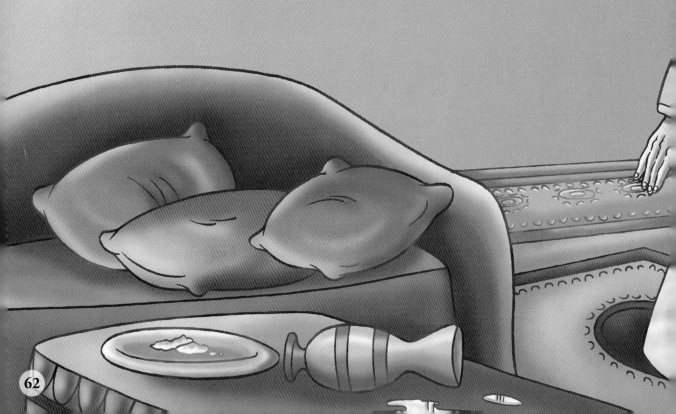

When he looked around for his wife, he found her having a bath. She was singing a merry tune while bathing; unaware of what was happening in the house.

Then it struck him that the parrot was not wrong. It was telling the truth.

The husband repented for his folly of not trusting the innocent parrot and punishing it.

A Bull and a Donkey

Once upon a time, there lived a farmer. He had a bull and a donkey in his farm.

The farmer had a special talent. He could understand the language of animals.

One evening, while he was giving food to the bull and donkey, he heard a conversation between them.

The bull said, "My friend, you are very lucky." The donkey looked surprisingly at

the bull. The bull continued, "Every morning, they put a heavy plough on my back and ask me to till the field. While all that is expected of you is to go to the washer man with clothes."

"The food I get in the evening is never enough for the kind of work they make me do through the day. And to think, they never allow me to rest," said the bull.

The donkey replied, "The problem is you are bright and chirpy every morning. Whereas, I always hang my head and walk slowly with the load on my back. So everyone always feels bad for me. Why don't you follow my plan and you will surely get a day's rest."

The bull was delighted. He said, "Sure! I will follow anything you say to laze around without work for a day!"

So the donkey told him his plan of acting sick the next morning.

The farmer had heard and understood this entire conversation. The bull and donkey were unaware of the farmer's talent, and slept peacefully that night, thinking that their plan would work the next day.

When the sun rose the next day, the bull suddenly acted sick. The farmer's helpers came to wake him up and give him food, but the bull kept lying down — his face hung to the ground!

So the helpers went back to the farmer and told him that the bull was unwell. They said that the tilling would have to be stopped that day.

The clever farmer knew what the problem was! So he told the helpers, "We cannot stop tilling the land. So, for today, put the plough on the donkey's back and continue tilling."

The helpers carried out the farmer's orders. The poor donkey tilled the land from morning to evening, while the bull lazed in the shed.

When the donkey came back home that evening, the bull said, "I owe this rest to you my friend. I feel so good today." The donkey replied, "Now I know why people make fun of my dull brains! I gave you an idea, not knowing that I would bear the fruit of it!"

And so the donkey went to sleep that night with bruises on his back, as a result of the wonderful idea he had given...

Contents

Reprinted 2009

Published by

Om KIDZ is an imprint of Om Books International

Corporate & Editorial Office
A-12, Sector 64, Noida - 201 301
Uttar Pradesh, India
Phone: +91-120-477 4100

Sales Office
4379/4B, Prakash House, Ansari Road
Darya Ganj, New Delhi - 110 002, India
Phone: +91-11-2326 3363, 2326 5303
Fax: +91-11-2327 8091

Email: sales@ombooks.com
Website: www.ombooks.com

ISBN 978-81-87107-93-4

Printed by Tien Wah (PTE) Ltd

10 9 8 7 6 5 4 3 2

Magical Journey of

Arabian Nights

An imprint of Om Books International

Aladdin and the Genie

There lived a mother and son in Persia, many years ago. The boy was called Aladdin. His father had passed away. Aladdin's mother could only make enough money to buy one meal a day.

Aladdin knew how poor they were. But he did not help his mother with her work. He would play all day long with his friends.

One day, while Aladdin was playing with his friends in the street, a scary looking man

came to him. He was wearing fine robes and looked very rich. He said, "Aladdin, you will not recognize me. I am your uncle. I have not seen you for years and thought I should visit your mother and you."

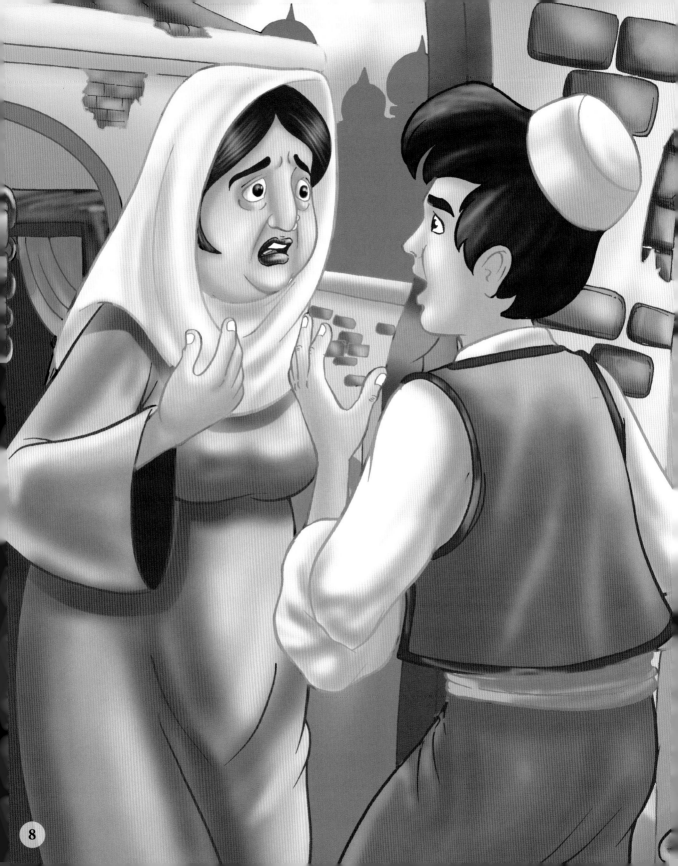

Aladdin was surprised. He said, "I have never heard of you!" The man replied, "Go and ask your mother whether you have an uncle or not. She will tell you."

Aladdin ran home excited. The moment his mother opened the door, he said, "Mom! You never told me that I have such a rich uncle!" Aladdin's mother did not understand what

he was saying. Then, when he explained his meeting the man on the street, she said, "I faintly remember your father talking about a brother."

The man visited Aladdin and his mother in the evening and showered them with gifts. Then he said, "Sister, I can understand your troubles and how difficult it is bringing up a

boy all by yourself. Send him with me and I will get him some great work." Aladdin and his mother had taken quite a liking for the man. So the next morning, Aladdin set out with his newly found uncle.

12

They traveled over mountains and valleys. Finally, they reached a mountain top. The man uttered some strange words and suddenly the rock parted and there appeared a hole, leading underground. Aladdin was shocked to

see all this. He realized that his uncle was no ordinary man and was a magician!

The magician said, "Aladdin, go down this hole and you will find an open door leading into three large halls. Pull your gown close to you. If any part of your clothing touches anything, you will die immediately. These halls lead into a garden of fine fruit trees. Keep walking past and you will come to a room where you will find a lighted lamp. Pour out the oil from the lamp and bring it to me."

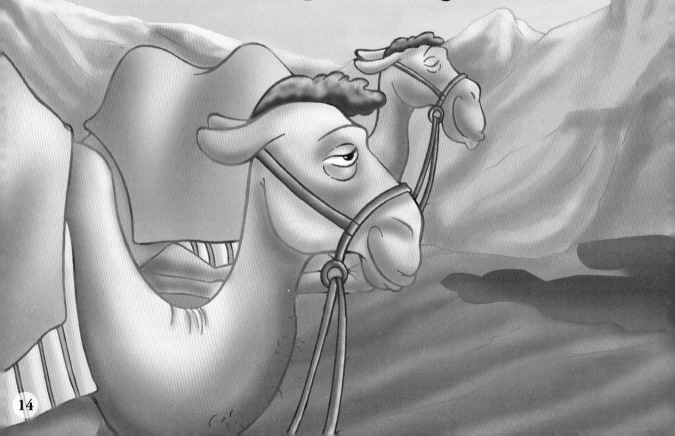

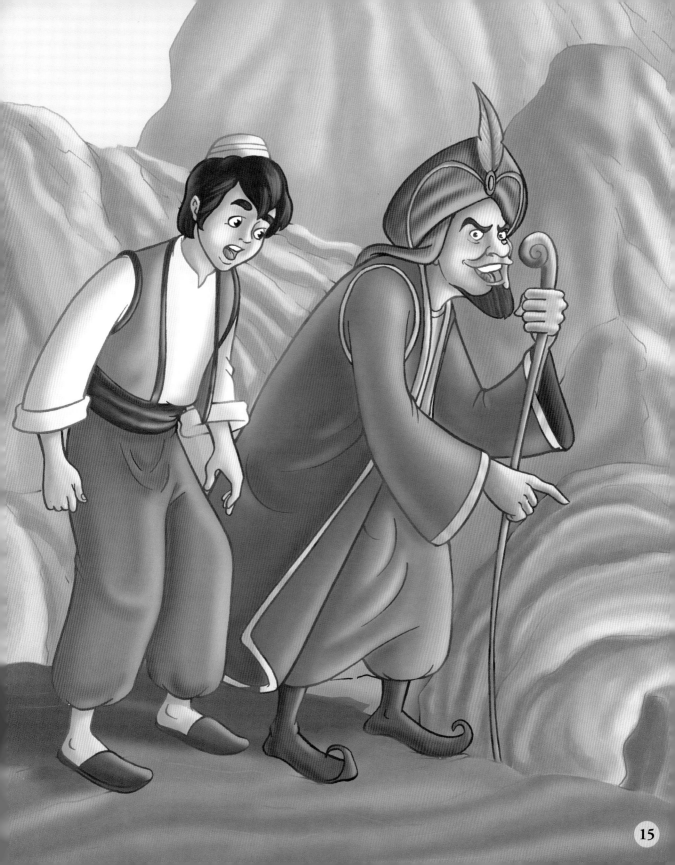

Then the magician pulled out a ring from his finger and gave it to Aladdin. He said, "Fear nothing and you are sure to prosper!" Aladdin then went down the hole. Just like the magician had said, there was an open

door, which he went past. He also walked past
the fruit trees.

Then he looked for the lamp. He found it
just at the place the magician had said it
would be. He poured out the oil and walked

back to the entrance of the hole. He then shouted out to the magician, "Pull me up! I have the lamp."

When the magician saw the lamp in Aladdin's hand, he said, "Hand me over the lamp!" Aladdin did not trust his uncle. He understood that all this was planned. So he replied, "Pull me out first and then I will give you the lamp." The magician was adamant about taking the lamp first. When Aladdin refused to give it, he closed the hole with a rock. Aladdin was trapped inside the hole!

The magician had found out through his magical powers that there was a lamp, which could make him the most powerful man in the world. But he could not get it on his own and had to find someone to do the task. So the evil magician had found Aladdin for getting him the lamp.

Poor Aladdin — trapped in the hole — cried for hours. Not knowing what to do, he clasped the lamp between his palms. While doing so, he rubbed the ring the magician had given him. Suddenly from nowhere, there was a big sound. Smoke arose from all over and strangely, the smoke seemed to take a shape. When Aladdin looked closely, he saw that the

smoke had formed into a huge creature. It was a genie!

The genie, "Master, I am at your service. I am the genie of the ring and I will appear whenever you rub it."

Aladdin was shocked. But he was soon delighted as he realized that the genie would do anything he asked. The genie asked Aladdin, "Tell me master, what is your command?"

Aladdin replied, "Get me out of this place."

Within seconds, he was transported out by the genie on a flying carpet and taken home to his mother. Such was the power of the genie of the ring.

When he reached home, his mother hugged him and said, "Aladdin! My son, where were you? I was so worried."

Aladdin told her all about his adventure with the magician. He then said, "Mom! I am hungry. Give me some food."

His mom replied, "Alas, my son, there is nothing in the house. I have spun some cotton and I will go and sell it in the market to fetch you some food." Aladdin said, "Instead of selling your cotton, why don't you sell this lamp?"

Aladdin's mother took a good look at the old lamp and started rubbing it to see what it was worth. Within seconds, another huge genie appeared, which said, "I am the genie of the lamp. What is your command, master?"

Aladdin's mother was weak hearted and fainted seeing the genie. But the fearless Aladdin said, "Get me food!"

The genie brought him the best of dishes — all in a jiffy! There were silver plates and silver

spoons for cutlery and the number of items on the table were more than what Aladdin and his mother could eat in a week.

Aladdin's mother told him, "Son, let us not have anything to do with devils. Sell the lamp and the ring." But Aladdin was adamant. He

said, "Now we know what the genies can do for us. We will always ask them to do good for us. Do not worry mother, everything will be fine."

The genies had changed their lives forever... . Aladdin and his mother lived happily for years.

Aladdin and Zebunissa

Aladdin was living happily with his mother, until one day, he heard an announcement by the Sultan's messengers about Princess Zebunissa passing his street everyday for her bath. They announced, "No window is to be open and no one is to see her!"

But, Aladdin, who was very curious to see Zebunissa hid behind the door to see her. When she lifted her veil, he saw how beautiful she was and fell in love with her that very moment! He begged his mother to ask for her hand from the Sultan.

Aladdin's mother was shocked, but realized how adamant her son was. So, she decided to see the Sultan in his audience chamber with a special gift. The Sultan did not take notice of her for almost a week, until one day, he gave her a chance. She told the Sultan, "Your

majesty, I have come to ask you for the hand of your lovely daughter."

The Sultan was surprised, but when Aladdin's mother showed him the precious jewels she had brought as a gift, he agreed. But the evil

Vazir, who wanted his son to marry Zebunissa, asked the Sultan to wait for three months, which he agreed upon. But within two months, the Sultan decided to marry the princess to the Vazir's son. Aladdin was very angry to hear this and shouted, "Mother, the Sultan has cheated me!"

So he summoned the genie and said, "Tonight, get the bride and the bridegroom to me." That night, the genie carried the bride and the bridegroom with their bed to Aladdin. He told the frightened princess, "Fear not! You are my wife, promised by your father to me." He then slept next to her, while the Vazir's son slept outside in the cold. The next morning, the genie took the bride and bridegroom back to the palace.

When Zebunissa spoke to her mother and father, she said, "I was carried to a different house. I spoke to a strange man who said he was my husband." Zebunissa's mother thought it was just a dream. But this happened every night.

When the three months of wait got over, Aladdin sent his mother to meet the Sultan again. This time the Sultan said, "I will remember my promise of marrying my daughter to your son if he can fulfill a small

condition. He has to send me forty basins of gold and jewels carried by forty slaves."

Aladdin summoned the genie and the Sultan got his basins of gold. The Sultan finally agreed to the wedding, but Aladdin asked for time to build a beautiful palace for the princess.

He summoned the genie and
said, "Build a palace of fine marble, precious
stones and gold." The genie got the palace
ready in a day, and the Sultan held a grand
wedding for the couple, who lived happily in
their lovely palace.

But, miles away, the evil magician remembered Aladdin, who came to know through his magic that he now lived happily with a lovely princess. He disguised himself as a trader, arrived in front of Aladdin's palace and shouted, "New lamps for old!" Zebunissa asked her handmaid to take the old lamp lying in her house to the trader and get a new one. Little did she know that it was the genie's lamp!

The magician was delighted to get the
genie's lamp. He rubbed the lamp and
commanded the genie to carry him, the
princess and the palace to another city.

When Aladdin returned from his hunting trip, he was very sad to find the palace and his wife missing. But, he remembered that he still had the genie of the ring. So he rubbed his ring and there came the genie! Aladdin commanded the genie to take him to Zebunissa, which the genie did.

Aladdin hugged his wife and asked her, "Where did you keep the lamp I left in the house?" Zebunissa replied, "I sold it to the evil magician, who now carries it with him all the time." Aladdin told her, "Be nice to him and

get it by tricking him." That night when the magician came to meet Zebunissa, she told him, "I have understood that Aladdin is dead. So I have decided to marry you. Let us drink to our lovely wedding!" So saying, she gave

him a goblet of wine, in which she had mixed a potion without the magician's knowledge. The magician was very happy to hear the news and drank the wine. After a few minutes, he fell to the ground as the potion took

effect. Aladdin jumped out of hiding and killed the magician.

Finally, the genie of the lamp brought Aladdin, Zebunissa and the palace back to where they belonged. Everyone lived happily ever after ...

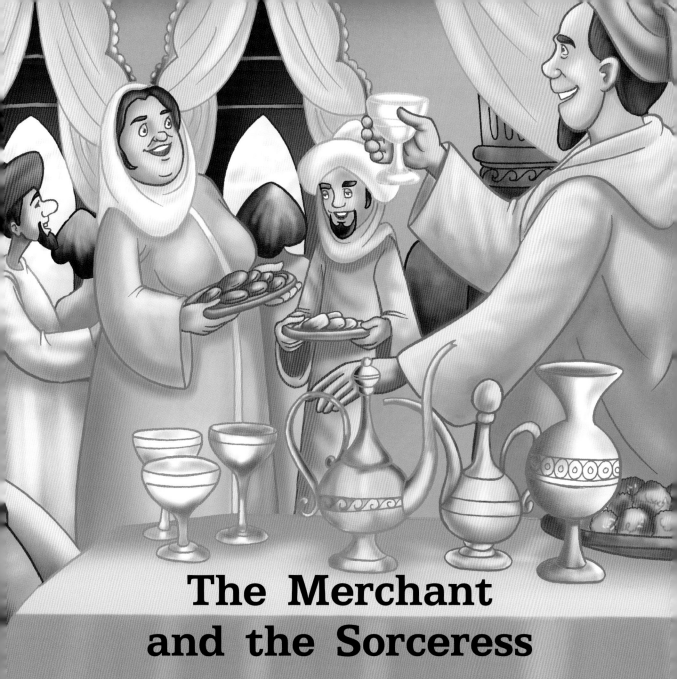

The Merchant
and the Sorceress

In the city of Baghdad lived a rich merchant. There was celebration everywhere in his house, as the merchant was getting married to a fair and beautiful lady by the name Amina.

The marriage took place with all pomp and splendour. A few nights after the marriage, the merchant invited his friends home for dinner. Amina — the newly wed bride — did not come out of her chamber for a long time.

When she finally came to the table, she sat alone at one end and refused to talk to anyone. The merchant told his friends, "Amina is very shy and takes time to mix with people. Feel no discomfort and enjoy yourselves!"

Everyone on the table was shocked to see what Amina ate during dinner. She merely picked a few grains of rice and put it into her mouth. The merchant kept urging her to eat more, but Amina would not listen.

A few days later, the merchant was having dinner alone with Amina. She repeated the same act of having only a few grains. The merchant told Amina, "Fair one, your appetite is less than that of a sparrow. Fear not about

ungainly weight. Eat and enjoy, as you are now the bride of one of the richest men in Baghdad!" But Amina would neither speak nor listen to him.

That night, the merchant kept a watch on Amina. A few hours past midnight, he saw her slip out of the bed and slowly walk towards the door. He followed her quietly. When he

reached the door, he saw Amina talking to an ogre. The merchant was shocked!

"How can Amina talk to an ogre?" wondered the merchant. He decided to follow Amina and the ogre. He finally saw them kill animals and eat them. The merchant realized that his bride was not a human being, but was a sorceress — a magician! And that too, an evil one!

The next day, at lunch, he decided to confront her. He said, "Amina, how can grains be as tasty as the animal blood?" Amina's face became red with anger. She picked up some powder in her hands and threw it at the merchant's face uttering a spell. Instantly, the merchant turned into a dog. Amina then drove the dog out of the house.

The merchant, in the form of the dog, wandered on the streets of Baghdad, not knowing how to get back his body. He then found a shopkeeper having a fight with an old lady.

The old lady was saying, "Why would I give you fake notes?" The shop keeper insisted that the money the lady had given was fake. Suddenly, the shop keeper's eyes fell on the

dog at the entrance. He told the lady, "The notes you have given are so fake, that even the dog can tell that." He called the dog inside. He then put an original note along side the fake note. He asked the dog to point out to the fake note. The dog, which was actually the merchant, recognized the fake note and pointed it out.

The shopkeeper, lady and all the people standing there were stunned to see the dog's ability. The shopkeeper decided to keep the dog with him.

Every morning he would put the dog at the counter and ask it to find fake notes and coins from what people gave him. The dog would do exactly that!

One morning, a lady dressed in odd clothes came to the shop. As usual, the merchant put the coins she gave in front of the dog and it pointed out the fake ones. The lady left with a smile. She went to the entrance of the shop and signaled to the dog to follow her.

The dog decided to follow the lady, hoping she could be the angel who would give it back the human shape.

The lady walked a long way, before reaching a small house. The dog entered the house along with the lady.

It heard the lady saying to a young girl, "Didn't I tell you that the dog that we have all heard about could be someone in a spell? See! Here it is!" The young girl in that room

picked up a powder and uttered a spell. She then threw it on the dog and within minutes, standing in that room was the merchant.

He was overjoyed! He shouted, "I am back! I am back! I have my body back!" He then

told the mother and daughter about Amina and her spell.

The young lady said, "I know your wife, Amina. We studied magic together. But she decided to use magic for evil purposes and I

chose to help out those who would be hurt by her."

The merchant replied, "How do I go home now? If Amina sees me, she will cause me more harm." The young lady calmed his

fears by giving him a powder and teaching him a spell.

The merchant went back to his house and hid behind the door. When Amina entered, he stepped ahead in front of her and not wasting

a second, threw the powder on her and shouted, "Pay the sins of your crimes!" Amina screamed and tried to run. But it was too late. She had turned into a horse!